Don't miss the other stories in the Ghost Detective short story series, some already published, some coming out in the next year or two:

Just Desserts
Lost Friends
Family Bonds
Till Death
Family History
Common Ground
Heritage
Eternal Bond
New Beginnings

R.W. WALLACE

Author of the Tolosa Mystery Series

JUST DESSERTS

A Ghost Detective Short Story

Just Desserts

by R.W. Wallace

Copyright © 2020 by R.W. Wallace

Copy editing by Jinxie Gervasio

All characters and events in this book, other than those clearly in the public domain, are fictitious and any resemblance to real persons, living or dead, is purely coincidental.

All rights reserved. No part of this publication may be reproduced, distributed, or transmitted in any form or by any means, including photocopying, recording, or other electronic or mechanical methods, without the prior written permission of the publisher, except in the case of brief quotations embodied in critical reviews and certain other noncommercial uses permitted by copyright law. For permission requests, write to the publisher, addressed "Attention: Permissions Coordinator," at the address below.

www.rwwallace.com

ISBN: [979-10-95707-13-4]

Main category—Fiction
Other category—Mystery

First Edition

14 13 12 11 10 / 10 9 8 7 6 5 4 3 2 1

Also by R.W. Wallace

Mystery

The Tolosa Mystery Series
The Red Brick Haze (free)
The Red Brick Cellars

Ghost Detective Shorts (coming soon)
Just Desserts
Lost Friends
Family Bonds
Common Ground

Short Stories
Critters
Gertrude and the Trojan Horse
First Impressions
Let Them Eat Cake
Out of Sight
Two's Company
Like Mother Like Daughter

Science Fiction (short stories)
The Vanguard

Lollapalooza Shorts
Quarantine
Common Enemies
Coiled Danger
Mars Meeting

Other short stories
Size Matters
Unexpected Consequences

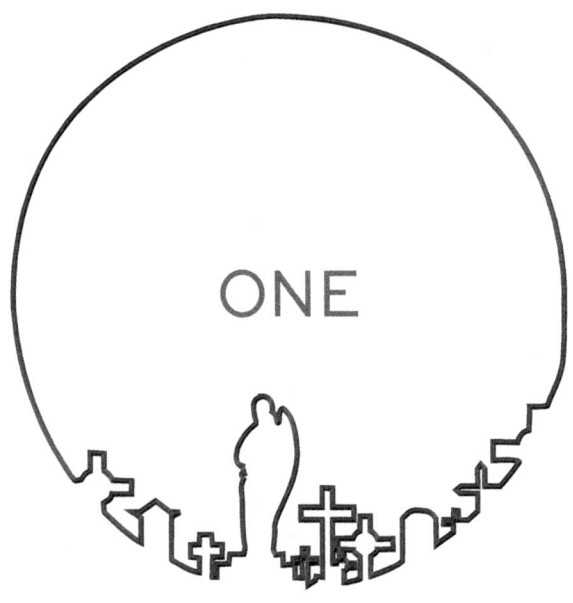

ONE

We hear the screams as soon as the group exits the church.

"I think this one's for you, Robert," Clothilde says. She's sitting on top of her tombstone, the plainest slab of stone in the whole graveyard, with only her first name and a date of death. No birthday, no last name, no citation or drawings of angels. She's one of the greatest mysteries this place has, but she won't let me investigate. Every attempt I've made to ask her about her life has been rebuffed, sometimes nicely, sometimes not so much. She's been dead for twenty-five years, but she'll always be a teenager at heart.

Today she's wearing high-waisted jeans that stop just above her ankle and a white top that would have shown the straps of her bra if she'd been wearing one. Her dangling feet are covered in a pair of Converse, worn on the heel and one of the laces torn on her right foot. There's no telling the color—the dead only wear shades of gray.

We haven't had many new arrivals lately. The only people to die were old ladies with no reason to hang around after the funeral. When you've known for years that your time is almost up, you get your shit together and make sure there are no loose ends.

It's those of us who are taken by surprise who linger.

Of course, it's a good thing when someone goes straight to the afterlife. None of us wish suffering on another human being—or human ghost in this case—but it does get a little dull at times. There's only so much you can do to occupy your time when you're stuck within the confines of your cemetery, and it's the middle of winter so the number of visitors is at a minimum.

Today, though, we have a new arrival.

It's not easy coming to grips with being dead when you didn't expect it, didn't see it coming. It's a bit of a shock, to put it mildly.

Personally, I pounded on my casket for a week before realizing my fists didn't have any effect on the sturdy wood. Nor did they make any sound. My voice didn't echo like it should have.

Only when I calmed down—if I can really call it that—did I look around in the small space I occupied. And realize I was lying next to my own dead body.

JUST DESSERTS

I was laid out on white sheets, wearing my next best suit—the best one would be full of holes to match the ones on my body—my hands folded over my stomach and my expression relaxed in a way I'd never seen it before.

I'm not particularly bright, so it took me another day to accept the fact that I was dead and had apparently become a ghost.

That's when the coffin released me. The cemetery has been my home ever since.

As the funeral procession advances down the path from the church, my fellow ghosts gather next to me. We always wait for the new arrivals by the hole in the ground that will be their last resting place. We could have listened in at the church door and followed the procession, but whenever a ghost touches a human, there can be a form of interaction, and we don't want to freak out the bereaved any more than they already are.

So we observe the funerals from behind the priest, in the trees, from the top of the tombs, watch the coffin lowered into the ground, and settle in to wait to see if a new companion would join us.

There isn't really any doubt about this one being a keeper.

The screams are so loud it would have been impossible for us to hear each other speak. The banging on the coffin is strong, panicked, and unrelenting. I can't make out any words, only pure, unadulterated panic.

I want to go over and calm her down, tell her it's going to be okay.

But as long as she hasn't been released from the coffin, there's nothing I can do. She won't hear me.

And it's not going to be okay.

She's dead and she wasn't ready.

A lot of people have come to see her off. I'm guessing close to a hundred, which for a little town like this, is quite impressive. At the front are a couple in their forties who I'm going to assume are her parents. A couple of grandparents. Two boys who might be brothers. Behind them, a group I'm going to qualify as family. There's a large majority of blondes, with strong jaws and wide shoulders. The darker-haired or darker-skinned ones have probably married in.

Slightly to the side, a mass of young people. Probably early twenties, and about eighty percent female. The friends.

Some are crying, some seem to not understand what's going on. Probably the first time they're burying someone they know that's not a grandparent. One guy at the back leans close to the guy next to him to say something and receives an extremely stern and accusing stare in return. Not the time for a joke, my man.

I don't listen to what the priest says. It's all to soothe the family and friends and won't have any interesting information for me.

I'm studying the mourners.

More than half of all murders are done by a family member. Add in the large group of friends and the probability of the murderer being in view is pretty darn high.

Judging by the screams coming from the coffin, the probability of her being a murder victim is also pretty darn high.

I sidle over to eavesdrop on a whispered conversation on the family side of the group. I'm going to guess cousins. One blond woman in her twenties is speaking into the ear of a second even blonder one.

"I can't believe her mom made such a big deal out of keeping it hidden that she killed herself," she whispers. "I mean, come on, is her image really that important? She can't own up to her daughter taking her own life?"

I glance in direction of the coffin with a frown. Suicide?

"It's not just the image thing," the second woman whispers back. "Julie has always been very involved in the church. If it's suicide, her daughter can't be buried in the cemetery."

Which is exactly why we have so few suicides in here. *Could* a ghost be that panicked after waking up from her own suicide? Shouldn't the situation be a tad more expected?

People who are aware that they are in mortal danger don't usually need much time to accept what happened and move on. A couple of years ago, we had a soldier who was killed in Afghanistan. He only lingered long enough to say goodbye to his girlfriend then disappeared in a puff of smoke.

"Well," says the first one, "luckily, falling off a bridge with no witnesses isn't automatically ruled as a suicide. So here we are."

I move on, listening to people saying they don't understand how it's possible, the service was beautiful, the mother had made an excellent choice for the casket, the soccer game starts in an hour and a half, will they be able to watch it?

That last one is from the guy making the inappropriate comment or joke earlier, and it earns him the same look from his neighbor. "Seriously, Joss. I know this isn't your scene, but can you at least just shut up?"

Joss the jokester shuts up, clamping his lips shut as if he wishes they could be glued together. Despite the cold, a bead of sweat trickles down along his hairline, past his ear, and into his shirt.

If he's a talker, I'm guessing we'll see him again. Possibly for a confession.

As the casket is lowered into the ground, I stand next to the guy I'm assuming is the husband or boyfriend. He's part of the friend group, but also right next to the parents. His eyes are red and a sob escapes on each breath. Arms hanging limply by his sides, twitching now and then.

He seems genuinely upset.

At least he doesn't have to hear the screams.

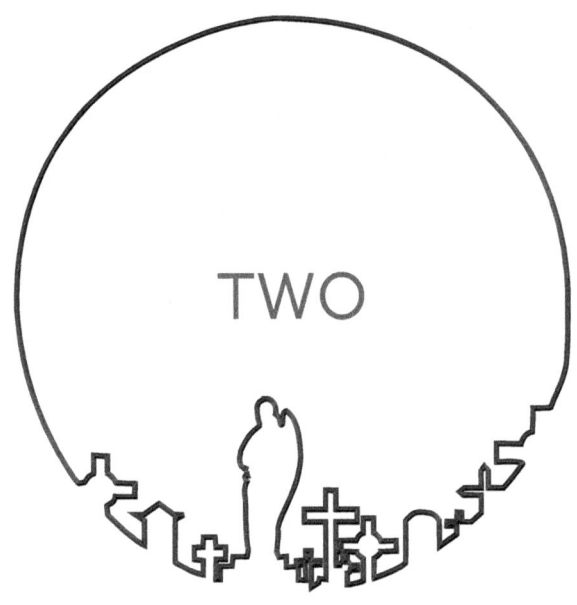

TWO

She's still screaming when her talkative and inappropriate jokester friend drops by two days later.

I'm visiting Clothilde, like I usually do when I'm on the lookout for visitors. None of us understand how she managed to afford a place in this cemetery in the first place, what with the no name, no family, no mourners thing, but at least there's a certain "logic" to hers being the least popular spot, right next to the trash by the exit.

The main entrance is on the other side, by the church, but that's not where the interesting visitors come through.

"So how long do you think she'll keep this up?" Clothilde asks as she lounges on the ground, right on top of where her casket lies, six feet below. Her hands folded behind her head and her ankles crossed, she stares dreamily at the two or three clouds clotting the painfully blue winter sky.

"I don't know," I reply. "Not much we can do about it. She'll just have to get it out of her system." I'm sitting with my back against her tombstone, arms around my bent knees, and my chin on my knees. I'd put my hands over my ears if I thought it would do any good.

Even if we do this regularly, it still grates on the nerves to hear someone screaming in panic from waking up in a coffin for several days on end.

Clothilde grunts and blows at a fly zipping around her nose. The fly careens off course.

"We can't all be like you," I say. "Accepting that you're dead isn't easy for anyone."

"It is if you were as good as dead before."

Clothilde tends to make cryptic and worrisome comments like this. There's no point in asking her to elaborate, she'll only clam up. But I take note of everything. One day, maybe, I'll understand where she came from.

The rusty hinges of the iron grate squeal and the jokester comes through. He looks more at ease in a pair of jeans and a thick leather jacket than he did in a suit two days ago, but there are dark circles under his eyes and his hair doesn't look like it's seen shampoo or a comb since the funeral.

He looks left and right, making sure he's alone—it's half past ten on a Wednesday night, of course he's alone—before making a beeline for the new grave.

"I'm going to listen in," I say as I jump up and follow. "You coming?"

Clothilde sighs. "Guess so." She rolls into an upright position with more grace than a dancer. "It'll take my mind off the screaming. Maybe."

The jokester stands at the limit between grass and dirt, his tear-filled eyes on the wooden cross with "Florence Bernard" penciled in. Just as I reach him, he falls to his knees in the dirt and the air goes out of his lungs in a *whoosh*.

He leans forward, shoving his hands into the black earth. His position makes me think of praying Muslims. But he's not talking to a deity. He's talking to the girl who's still screaming, who still hasn't accepted her fate.

"I'm so sorry," he sobs. "It's all my fault. I'm so, so sorry."

Ah. A confession.

Although I don't have the satisfaction of having worked to find the culprit, at least I can tell the girl about it when she comes out. Perhaps it will be enough to allow her to move on immediately.

"I told them, Flo," the man continues, his face only millimeters from touching the dirt. "I told them who did it, but they didn't believe me. Two different police officers and they told me to take a hike. I didn't even make a joke!"

He sobs for a couple of minutes. His hands start to shake, probably from the biting cold, but he leaves them buried.

"This is why I always make the jokes, Flo. Nobody ever takes me seriously, so I might as well make it look like it's on purpose. You were the only one to ever really listen to me. And now you're dead because of that *bastard*!" A fist escapes the dirt and he slams it into the ground several times, gasps escaping as his body attempts to sob and breathe at the same time.

Okay, so maybe he's not the killer. It would be really helpful if he could give me a name, though. This is where being a ghost is really a drag—my suspects can't hear my questions.

"Everybody can see how much he loved her." He's quoting someone, complete with dirty fingers slashing quote marks in the air. "He'd never lay a hand on her. Can't you see how torn up he is? Of *course* he's torn up! He bloody killed you! He no longer has his golden goose!"

He sits back on his haunches and runs his hands through his hair. I wince in sympathy and hope he's planned on taking a shower soon.

I also wish he'd give me a *name*.

The man calms down. He pats the dirt back into place, as if having a perfectly smooth mound of dirt is Flo's greatest preoccupation at the moment.

"You shouldn't have done it," he says, his voice so low I can hardly hear him over his friend's screams. "We were *fine* as just friends. Worked out really well. You had your successful fiancé, the great job, the white picket fence in view. Everything you and your father had planned for."

He sits back on his heels. "Shouldn't have thrown it all away, Flo. I'd rather have had you for a friend than not have you at all."

Okay. Moving the fiancé up to the top of the list of suspects.

The friend—lover?—stays for over an hour, crying silently on the grave.

The screams from below continue.

THREE

It takes her ten days to come to terms with it. I'd say she's slow, but I was no better.

When the screams stop on the eighth day, I set up camp on top of her grave, right in front of the wooden cross, waiting for her to show her face. I'm a little leery of what I'll see.

I've seen quite a few horrors since I arrived in this cemetery, not to mention while I was alive, but it still affects me. If she died in the water, the question is how long it took before she was found. Some ghosts retain the form they had while they lived. A few of the senile ones are lucky enough to take a younger form of their bodies since it's all they can remember.

And some, the ones who stay dead for too long before becoming ghosts, walk around with cut up or bloated or maimed bodies, reminding everyone of their violent demise.

Florence, luckily, has retained the body from before she ended up in the river.

At sunset, her head breaks through the mound of dirt first, followed by two hands. She brings her arms up above her head, then lets them fall back down, watching how they aren't affected by the dirt.

She jerks when she sees me sitting on the ground in front of her but doesn't seem to tag me as a threat. "I'm a ghost," she says. It's a mixture of a question and a challenge, letting me decide if I want to answer or be scared.

"I know," I reply. "So am I."

She studies me closer, takes in the lack of color, the slight transparency that's more obvious during the day, my out-of-date fashion sense. She nods.

She waves her hands through the dirt again. "How come you're sitting on top of the ground and I'm stuck inside it? What am I even standing on? The coffin?" Her voice breaks on the last word.

"You're probably on the coffin, yes." I stand up and offer her a hand. "You can climb out on your own if you want, but I'm more than happy to help."

She eyes my hand, trying to decide if she can trust me.

"It's up to you to decide if you want things to be real to you or not. If you expect the dirt to have steps to help you get out, it will. If you expect it to let you pass through, it will. You'll get the hang of it pretty quickly."

A frown appearing on her too-young forehead, she studies the dirt as if it has personally offended her. Then she takes a step forward and up, as if she's walking up a set of stairs.

She's a quick study, this one.

She stands in front of me, looking around at our cemetery. I can hardly remember what I thought of it the first time I saw it. Now it's just my home, with the high stone walls cutting us off from the living world, the relatively small stone church with its seven bells, and the six hundred and seventy-seven graves. Some are mausoleums with pictures and statues of angels and seats for visitors, some simple tombstones with only a name on them.

She turns her sharp gaze on me. "Now what?"

I clear my throat and straighten my spine. Nobody gave me this job, nobody asked me to do it. I've decided to do it because I want to.

Because I think I have to.

I help the newcomers get settled, understand how things work. I help them find the closure they need to move on.

The closure I'm not sure I'll ever find for myself.

"The reason you're here as a ghost," I explain, "is that you have unfinished business. Once it's done, you can move on."

"Move on to where?"

I spread my hands wide. "That, I cannot say. I'm afraid I haven't made it that far myself yet. Hence my continued presence. I assume, though, that it is a better place. It is what we strive for."

She chews on her lip as she digests this. A speck of dirt that had stayed on her shoulder falls through her body and to the ground. She probably forgot that she's supposed to be covered in dirt after walking out of her grave.

"What kind of unfinished business?"

"Well." I clear my throat though there hasn't been a need to for a good thirty years. "It appears you were murdered. I'm guessing we're looking for the killer."

She doesn't appear surprised to hear she was murdered. "We?" she asks.

I crack a smile. "As you can see, there aren't that many things to do here. It would be my pleasure to help you out."

She nods. "So, we do what? Go haunt places?"

"Ah. I'm afraid we're very limited when it comes to haunting. We can't leave the cemetery grounds, you see. So we can only haunt whoever deigns to come visit us."

I see she's about to lash out. "I wouldn't worry overly much, my dear," I tell her. "You've only been in the ground for ten days and only one man has come to see you. There will be others." Possibly not before the tombstone is in place, though. People seem to prefer visiting a clean grave to a mound of dirt. Don't ask me why.

"Who came?" she asks, a first trace of vulnerability making an appearance. "Was it Joss?"

"I believe that was his name, yes," I tell her. I describe the man as best I can. "I got the feeling he was a good friend?"

Her clear eyes look toward the church with longing. "More than a friend. Or at least, that was the plan."

"Do you know who pushed you off that bridge?" I ask. "I assume you didn't jump?"

"Of course I didn't jump," she snaps. "I was finally going after what I wanted instead of what my father had planned for me. I was finally going to *live*." She takes a few deep breaths—a habit most of us keep even though we don't actually breathe anymore—before continuing in a calmer voice. "And no, I don't know who it was."

"What do you remember?"

She'd been on the bridge by herself, staring at the dark waters below, like she often did when she needed a time out. It was her spot, and everyone who was even remotely close to her knew it. She'd been listening to music, so she hadn't heard anyone approach. One minute she'd been listening to Beyoncé. The next she was flying through the air, seeing the water and the rocks below coming to meet her as she fell face first to her death.

"All right," I say. "So we don't know who the killer is. The good part is it means that might be all you need to be able to move on. Figure out who killed you, and we're done."

She studies me, skepticism clear on her youthful and pretty face. "What's in this for you? Why do you want to get me out of here? Am I stepping on your turf or something?"

I laugh, but it sounds hollow. "You're welcome to stay here with me as long as you like, Florence. I'd be happy for the company. But believe me when I say this: you do not want to stay here forever. It gets *very* boring. And the longer you wait, the more difficult it is to do what you have to do, and you risk ending up staying here forever."

She studies me, making me want to fidget. I can see the question in her eyes, but I'm grateful when she doesn't give it voice.

Yes, I suspect I'll be here forever. And yes, that scares me. But keeping busy assisting the others helps.

The hinges of the back gate squeak and I breathe a sigh of relief when Florence turns her focus toward the sound.

"Looks like we can start the work straight away, my friend," she says. "That's my fiancé."

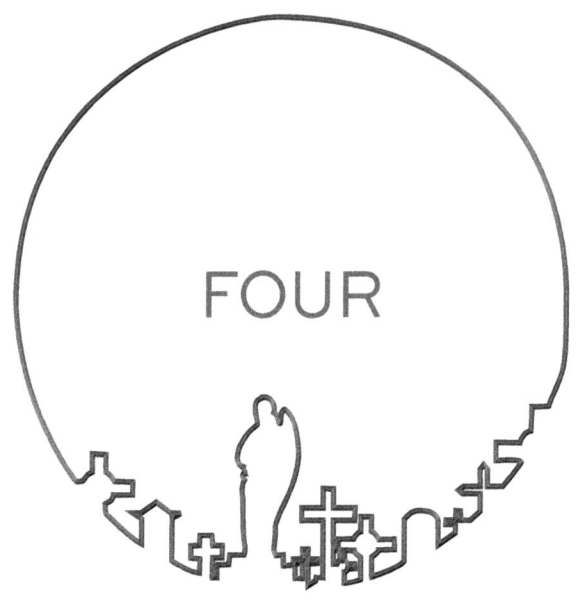

FOUR

The young man who'd stood at the limit between family and friends at the funeral gently closes the gate behind him, wincing at the resulting squeak. Hands shoved into the pockets of his fancy leather winter jacket, he approaches Flo's grave, his steps hesitant.

"I assume he can't see me?" Flo asks.

I shake my head.

"Hear? Feel?"

I tip my head from side to side. "Not like you're used to, no. But they do feel *something*." I wave a hand at the fiancé, who's almost at the mound of dirt. "Go ahead and experiment."

I'm guessing we'll need it if we want a confession out of him before he leaves the premises.

Flo sidles up to her fiancé's side. "Hey, Cédric." She cocks her head to look up at him.

"Hey, Flo."

Flo jumps a foot into the air and wide eyes meet mine. "You said he wouldn't hear me!"

I have to crack a smile. "He didn't," I assure her. "He's talking to your grave, that's all."

"I'm not sure why I came tonight." Cédric talks to the wooden cross, his hands still in his pockets and his shoulders drawn up so the collar of his jacket covers his ears. I don't know the man, but his voice feels flat, lifeless.

Flo steps in front of her fiancé, probably so it feels like he's looking at her. "What did you do, Cédric?"

I like this girl. She knows he can't really hear her, but my comment about them feeling something has her asking questions anyway. The thing is, I think it does help. They don't hear our actual words, but on some unconscious level, they must hear us, because two times out of three, they change the course of their monologue in the direction we want.

Cédric draws an uneven breath. "I swear I didn't know this was how it would end up. You must know I'd never do anything to hurt you."

"You didn't know how this would end up." Flo seems to taste the words in her mouth, trying them on to see if they fit. She turns to look at me. "That doesn't feel quite right if he pushed me off the bridge, does it?"

I shift my weight to my right foot and fold my arms across my chest. "Not really, no. But I'd like firmer proof."

She nods. "What did you do, Cédric?" she asks him again.

He shakes his head, tears filling his eyes. "I was just so hurt by what you did, Flo. After everything we'd built together, all the plans we'd laid. How could you just throw that away—for *Joss*?"

Flo raises a hand to his cheek—and her hand goes right through his head.

"You need to focus on the space he occupies," I tell her. "Expect to touch him, and you will." Sort of.

After shaking off a shiver, Flo tries again. This time, her hand caresses his cheek, though from the twitch in her fingers, I'm guessing she's freaked out by the lack of feeling.

"I'm so sorry I hurt you," Flo tells him. "But what we had was always more of a business agreement than a relationship. And I couldn't take it anymore."

"I guess I shouldn't be surprised," Cédric says. "Passion was never really our thing, was it?" He raises his eyes to the stars above us. "But *Joss*?"

Flo gives an annoyed sigh. "You're just going to have to get over that one, Cédric. But I am sorry for using you, even if I wasn't aware of doing it." She braces herself, then gives him a whole-body hug. Does it well, too. Not a single piece of her goes through the man.

I'd say he feels it. He visibly relaxes, his shoulders going down a fraction.

"What did you do, Cédric?" Flo lets her fiancé go, and steps back to stand in his line of sight again.

"Why'd you do it, Flo?" Cédric says.

Flo takes a step backward. "Why did I do what?"

A tear streaks down Cédric's face and disappears into his collar. "I get that your dad was probably pissed, but you're a strong girl. I mean, you *knew* he'd be unhappy about us breaking the engagement. Was that really enough to give up?" His shoulders slump and two more tears break free. "I just don't get it."

Flo's body is frozen to the spot. She turns her head just enough to look at me out of the corner of her eye. "What is he talking about?"

I remember the conversation between cousins at the funeral. "There's a chance people think you killed yourself."

"What!" Her head whips back and forth as she's trying to stare daggers at me and her fiancé both. "I would never do that!"

I step closer so she can look at both of us without giving herself the ghost equivalent of a whiplash. "I'm guessing this is the business you need to take care of before you can leave." I give her fiancé a once-over. "This man was at the top of my list of suspects, but for what we're seeing, I don't think he did it. Unless he's managed to convince himself you jumped of your own accord after he did the deed?"

Flo shakes her head. "Not his style."

Cédric falls to his knees, tears running freely now. He hangs his head as he sobs but doesn't seem to have the intention of talking any more.

"Let's look at this objectively," I say. "We know it's not the fiancé, and it's not the lover. Who else could it be? What could be the motive?"

Flo runs ran a hand through Cédric's hair, shivers and looks accusingly at her hand as if it is at fault for not giving her the usual feedback when she touches something.

"The motive is probably money," she says reluctantly. "I was planning on breaking it off with Cédric, but also getting out of the family business. I told him he could continue working with my dad, but I didn't want to do it anymore. I'm—I *was*—the face outward for our company. My dad thought, and rightly so, that having a young woman at the front of a business catering to mostly men would be good business. So if I'm no longer there, they will have to rework the entire business plan."

"Doesn't exactly point toward your competitors," I say. "If you were leaving anyway."

She shrugs. "Not many people knew, so maybe they just decided to make their move exactly when there was no need?"

I chew on my lip. "I guess it's possible. But I'm tempted to say it's someone from your side of things. Someone who wasn't happy about you leaving."

Flo points to the man sobbing at our feet. "He was the only one who knew. And Joss." Worry etches her forehead. "You're *sure* it wasn't Joss, right?"

"I'm sure."

She lets out a relieved sigh.

"Could either one of them have told anyone else?" I ask.

Flo pulls a hand through her hair as she thinks. "Joss didn't have anything to do with the business. Nor did the friends he hung out with. He's never even met my dad."

"So your dad is the one to run everything? The big boss?"

She nods.

"The one who has the most to lose if you left the company?"

Her eyes snap to mine. "He wouldn't."

"It does sound far-fetched," I agree. "But I didn't know the man. How was he usually in stressful situations? How did he manage his anger?"

Her lips twitch, and for a couple of seconds, she's about six years old and wearing a cute princess dress. Then she's back to her twenty-year-old self.

"What happened when you were a little girl?" I ask her gently. "When you were dressed up like a princess?"

Flo's breathing is shallow. Her eyes are distant, probably looking back at whatever happened that day.

"I ruined the car," she whispers. "I was dancing in circles on the terrace and stumbled. I knocked into a jar of paint that stood on the railing and it fell down on the car. Made a dent in the roof and he had to get a new paint job for the whole thing afterward."

I put a hand on her shoulder. She won't be able to feel it, but I'm hoping her memory can fill in when she has the visual. "What did he do to you?"

She squeezes her eyes shut. "He held me over the railing, yelling at me to look at what I'd done. Said he'd drop me, that maybe then I'd learn my lesson."

"Did he? Drop you?"

She shakes her head. "My mom came out of the kitchen and saw us. Had him put me down and yelled at him for an hour for putting me in danger like that."

"How do you think he'd react to learning you intended to leave him in the lurch?"

Flo takes a deep breath and lets it out slowly. She looks down at her fiancé, who's stopped crying but shows no sign of leaving. "I need to know if my dad knew," she says. "How can we find out?"

"There's a good chance he'll confess to it himself if he comes here by himself," I reply. "And they usually do, after a time. So we'd just have to wait." I meet her gaze. "The question is whether or not that will be enough for you to move on. Do you think *you* knowing will be enough, or do the people who are still alive have to know, too?"

She runs her hand through the hair of her wreck of a fiancé, without twitching this time. "They need to know," she whispers.

"That's what I figured," I say. "It means you have some work to do."

Flo straightens her back and sets her jaw. "Tell me what to do."

I point to the man at her feet. "You need to convince him to help you."

FIVE

"How long to do you think this is going to take?" Clothilde asks from her perch. Where I usually try to respect the physical laws of the living, Clothilde doesn't care. She's standing on thin air to get a view of the parking lot over the wall.

I glance at the newly installed mausoleum over Flo's grave, with its brilliant gold letters and shiny surface. "Any day now." The mom came by this morning, and Flo cried as many tears as her mom during the encounter. The dad was absent, though, and the mother promised he'd drop in soon.

He'll be here soon. The question is whether or not he'll have a tail.

"Ah," Clothilde says. "A Ferrari. Haven't seen it before. Might be our guy."

I rise from my seat and walk over to the main entrance, where Flo is waiting. "Your father?" I ask.

She nods.

Showtime.

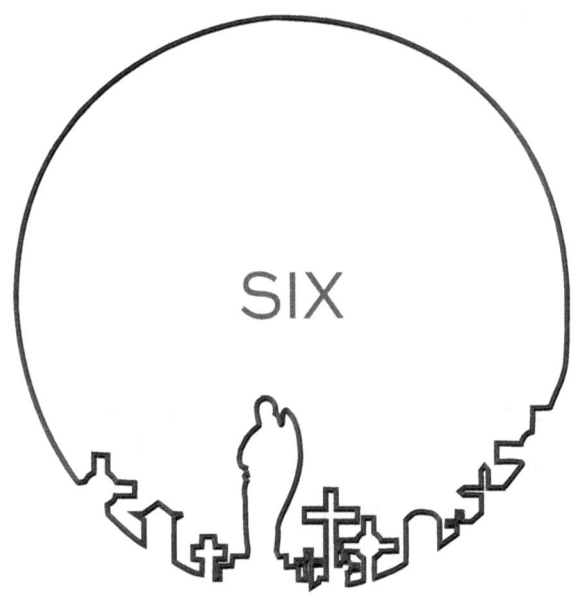

SIX

THE DAD TAKES his time getting out of the car. He walks to the passenger side to get his winter jacket and is careful with his suit at he slips it on. He strolls to the trunk, where he pulls out a bouquet of red roses.

"Mom bought them for him yesterday," Flo says. "She told me. Didn't want him to come empty-handed."

Fair enough. Not all men feel comfortable buying flowers.

The Ferrari is the only car in the parking lot. It might be happenstance, but if our suspicions are correct, he'd want to be alone today.

"A car just parked down the road toward the school," Clothilde informs me as she trots up to join us at the main entrance. "A blue Ford."

Flo's eyes light up. "That's Cédric! He listened!"

"Looks like it," Clothilde confirms. "I'll go meet him and see what I can do about those rusty hinges at the back door. But if he's no good at stealth, there isn't much I can do."

"Thank you," Flo says and squeezes the other girl's hand. I wouldn't go so far as to say they've become friends over the last week, but Clothilde seems invested in helping Flo get justice, and Flo knows to show her appreciation.

The dad looks around the parking lot as he approaches the main gate, and again when he's in the cemetery. Yup, definitely wanted to be alone. A Tuesday night at eleven is a good bet if that's what you want.

"Hey, Dad," Flo says as he passes us. "Long time, no see."

The dad stalks up the main path in direction of his daughter's grave. His expression is severe, not a tear in sight, his lips set in a thin line.

We follow in his wake, making sure to stay close enough to hear if he starts talking.

At the mausoleum, he sets the flowers down on the doorstep, then takes a step back. He takes his time in studying the little stone building set up in memory of his daughter but doesn't voice his thoughts about it. From his expression, I'd say he's not impressed.

Clothilde appears through the stone walls, hands raised and eyes wide. "Boo!" she says, then cackles a laugh. "Man, I wish that worked sometimes."

Flo's dad, of course, doesn't react at all.

Clothilde comes to stand with Flo and myself. "He climbed over the gate," she says, her voice impressed. "Tore open his pants and all but made it in without making a sound. He's hiding behind this horror, phone in hand." She points to the mausoleum.

"Guess it's my turn to play, then." Flo squares her shoulders and steps onto the first step of her new home, facing her father.

"Tell me, Dad," she says, her voice strong, "did someone tell you I was leaving?"

Her father grits his teeth and lets out a frustrated sigh. "Why did you have to do it?" he asks. "Why couldn't you stay on course? You were going to give up everything we'd worked for for *love*? Really? Give up a bright future with all the money and stability you could ever want, to go live with a guy who can't hold onto a job for more than six months?"

"Okay." Flo's eyes have lost some of their spark, but the determination is strong. "Someone told you. Guess it's not really important if it was Joss or Cédric, though I'm going to guess Cédric since I actually managed to convince him to follow you here." Joss had been by several times since she'd come out of the grave, and she'd talked to him about following her father, but to no effect.

"And now I even had to pay for *this*." Her dad kicks at the mausoleum, missing his daughter's ghost by mere millimeters.

"I'm sorry I'm always such a burden to you," Flo says. Her form flashes quickly to that of a much younger version of herself, then comes back to the version I know, anger flashing in her eyes. "At least you're rid of me now."

"At least I'm rid of you now," he echoes.

"Creepy," Clothilde whispers.

"Cédric came to me *crying*," the dad says, his own temper rising. "A grown man was crying in my lap because my daughter decided she didn't want him anymore. You take away everything we've worked for for *years*, and to top it all off, you break the one asset I could still use. What use is a man who starts *crying* over a *woman*?"

Clothilde takes off toward the back of the mausoleum. "I'm just going to check our little witness isn't going to do anything stupid until we have some definite proof."

"I can think of plenty of uses," Flo screams at him. "Cédric is a good man! He deserves a good life." She deflates a little and her voice lowers. "I couldn't give that to him. He might be sad right now, but I would have made him miserable in the long run."

"I was going to talk some sense into you," the dad says with a sneer. "Always standing on that bridge, wasting your time with God knows what. You'd just *sunk* my business, and there you were, *singing* and *shaking your ass* as if you were some ninny on TV who couldn't find anything more constructive to do with your time."

"I'm allowed to live my own life as I see fit!" Flo stands on her tiptoes, screaming into his face from no more than a centimeter away.

He flinches and takes a step back. He scans the cemetery but doesn't seem to see any of us standing around him, least of all his daughter right in front of him.

"Jeez," he says. "I'm even seeing things. See what you've brought me to? I'm staying up all night to work on finding your replacement, on finding a new marketing strategy. On figuring out what to do with that lousy fiancé of yours. And all because you can't bloody swim!" His voice rose throughout his speech and at the end he's screaming so loud, I'm surprised the neighbors don't come running.

"I can't swim?" Flo has taken a leaf out of Clothilde's book and is standing on thin air to get right into her father's face. "I can't swim? You know bloody well I can swim, since you insisted I learn when I was five! But I can't swim if my head's bashed in, Dad! I can't swim if I'm already dead! You did it, didn't you? You pushed me over the railing during one of your hissy fits, never thinking about the consequences of your actions!"

"Of course I did! You were just standing there, dancing, when everything was going to *shit*! You deserved to be thrown in! You deserved to pay the consequences! But you weren't supposed to die!"

Silence falls on the cemetery like a heavy brick.

"He just answered her question," Clothilde whispers as she pops her head around the mausoleum to meet my gaze.

"I know," I whisper back.

"Florence?" the dad asks, his voice shaky. He's looking right at her, not through her.

Flo's eyes are huge and her lips twitch as if she's about to start crying. "Daddy?"

The dad's eyes boggle, then roll to the back of his head. He falls to the ground like someone pressed his "off" button.

Cédric comes scrambling out from his hiding place. He takes in the flowers, the man sprawled on the ground. He's searching for something else, but he can't see the three of us crowding around him. "What the hell just happened?"

SEVEN

We stand by as the ambulance shows up and carts the father off on a gurney. While talking to the EMT, Cédric mentions what he'd overheard at Flo's grave and the police are called in. He shows them his recording.

"So it really wasn't a suicide, huh?" one of the officers says. "Good job on getting the evidence, kid."

After a while, even Joss shows up, and after a long discussion with Cédric where Flo listens in but I keep my distance, the two share a hug and leave together. There's not a dry eye in sight.

When there's only us ghosts left, and the cemetery is back to its usual silence, Flo approaches. She's still here, but I can see straight through her as she's becoming more translucent.

"Ready to leave?" I ask her.

"You think I'm done?" she asks. "How do I know if it's enough?"

I smile at her and lean in for a hug while it's still possible. As I step back, I wave a hand to indicate her body. "You're already on your way," I tell her.

She looks down at herself, at the fact that she can see through her legs, her torso, as if she's only just a memory of herself.

"Oh," she says in wonder. "Thank you." Her eyes are on mine as she disappears altogether.

I walk over to Clothilde's grave, where she's sitting, her legs dangling with her worn Converse going straight through the stone on every swing.

"Nice job, detective," she says. She makes a show of looking me over. "Still not enough?"

I sigh as I sit down on my own grave—a slight hump on the ground next to Clothilde's, without so much as a temporary cross to mark it. "I'm not sure it will ever be enough."

SEVEN

WE STAND BY as the ambulance shows up and carts the father off on a gurney. While talking to the EMT, Cédric mentions what he'd overheard at Flo's grave and the police are called in. He shows them his recording.

"So it really wasn't a suicide, huh?" one of the officers says. "Good job on getting the evidence, kid."

After a while, even Joss shows up, and after a long discussion with Cédric where Flo listens in but I keep my distance, the two share a hug and leave together. There's not a dry eye in sight.

When there's only us ghosts left, and the cemetery is back to its usual silence, Flo approaches. She's still here, but I can see straight through her as she's becoming more translucent.

"Ready to leave?" I ask her.

"You think I'm done?" she asks. "How do I know if it's enough?"

I smile at her and lean in for a hug while it's still possible. As I step back, I wave a hand to indicate her body. "You're already on your way," I tell her.

She looks down at herself, at the fact that she can see through her legs, her torso, as if she's only just a memory of herself.

"Oh," she says in wonder. "Thank you." Her eyes are on mine as she disappears altogether.

I walk over to Clothilde's grave, where she's sitting, her legs dangling with her worn Converse going straight through the stone on every swing.

"Nice job, detective," she says. She makes a show of looking me over. "Still not enough?"

I sigh as I sit down on my own grave—a slight hump on the ground next to Clothilde's, without so much as a temporary cross to mark it. "I'm not sure it will ever be enough."

THANK YOU

THANK YOU FOR reading *Just Desserts*. I hope you enjoyed it!

This story is the first of a series. I had a blast writing this first one and didn't really want to let Robert and Clothilde go straight away, so there are at least seven more short stories coming. Almost all will first be published in *Pulphouse Magazine*.

I'm also working on a novel series for my ghost detective, one where I bust him and Clothilde out of their cemetery. I'm having so much fun writing it and am looking forward to sharing them with you very soon.

If you liked the the story, you might want to check out some of my other books mentioned on the next page. It's mostly Mysteries, but a few other genre short stories will pop up, too.

And don't forget that the first book of my *Tolosa Mystery* series, *The Red Brick Haze*, is available for free on my website.

R.W. Wallace
www.rwwallace.com

Also by R.W. Wallace

Mystery

The Tolosa Mystery Series
The Red Brick Haze (free)
The Red Brick Cellars
The Red Brick Basilica

Ghost Detective Shorts (coming soon)
Just Desserts
Lost Friends
Family Bonds
Till Death
Family History
Common Ground
Heritage
Eternal Bond
New Beginnings

Short Stories
Hidden Horrors
Critters
Gertrude and the Trojan Horse
First Impressions
Let Them Eat Cake
Out of Sight
Two's Company
Like Mother Like Daughter

Urban Fantasy (short stories)
Unexpected Consequences
Morbier Impossible
A Second Chance

SCIENCE FICTION (SHORT STORIES)
The Vanguard

LOLLAPALOOZA SHORTS
Quarantine
Common Enemies
Coiled Danger
Mars Meeting

ADVENTURE (SHORT STORIES)
Size Matters

ABOUT THE AUTHOR

R.W. WALLACE WRITES in most genres, though she tends to end up in mystery more often than not. Dead bodies keep popping up all over the place whenever she sits down in front of her keyboard.

The stories mostly take place in Norway or France; the country she was born in and the one that has been her home for two decades. Don't ask her why she writes in English—she won't have a sensible answer for you.

Her Ghost Detective short story series appears in *Pulphouse Magazine*, starting in issue #9.

You can find all her books, long and short, all genres, on rwwallace.com.

www.ingramcontent.com/pod-product-compliance
Lightning Source LLC
LaVergne TN
LVHW051922060526
838201LV00060B/4133